The world's best
KNOCK KNOCK
JOKES for kids
VOLUME 4

Every single one
illustrated

SWERLING & LAZAR

Andrews McMeel
PUBLISHING®

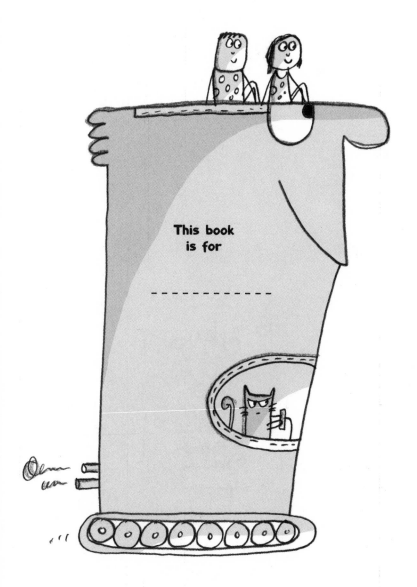

This book
is for

- - - - - - - - - -

DANGER!
This book contains
a lot of ridiculous,
sidesplittingly
funny, silly
JOKES!

Knock knock.
Who's there?

Goat.

Goat who?

Goat to the door and find out!

Knock knock.
Who's there?

Lena.

Lena who?

Lena little closer and I'll tell you.

Knock knock.
Who's there?

Hoo.

Hoo who?

Is there an owl in this house?

Knock knock.
Who's there?

Doris.

Doris who?

Doris locked! Open up!

Knock knock.
Who's there?

Howard.
Howard who?

Howard I know?

Knock knock.
Who's there?

Voodoo.
Voodoo who?

*Voodoo you think you are,
asking me so many questions?*

Knock knock.
Who's there?

Frank.

Frank who?

Frank you for being my friend.

Knock knock.
Who's there?

I smell mop.

I smell mop who?

Ewwwww, that's disgusting!

Knock knock.
Who's there?

Mustache.

Mustache who?

Mustache you a question,
but I'll shave it till later.

Knock knock.
Who's there?

Atch.

Atch who?

Bless you!

Achoo!

Knock knock.
Who's there?

Figs.

Figs who?

*Figs the doorbell,
it's broken!*

Knock knock.
Who's there?

Olive.

Olive who?

*Olive next
door—hello,
neighbor!*

Knock knock.
Who's there?

Candice.

Candice who?

*Candice door
open or not?*

9

Knock knock.
Who's there?

Ketchup.

Ketchup who?

Ketchup with me if you can,
and I'll tell you!

Knock knock.
Who's there?

Boo.

Boo who?

Sorry, I didn't mean to make you cry. It's just me!

Knock knock.
Who's there?

Ken.

Ken who?

Ken I come in? I really need the bathroom!

Knock knock.
Who's there?

Tyrone.

Tyrone who?

Tyrone shoelaces!

Knock knock.
Who's there?   Robin.

Robin who?

Robin' YOU! Now hand over the cash!

Knock knock.
Who's there?

Nana.

Nana who?

Nana
your business!

Knock knock.
Who's there?

Police.

Police who?

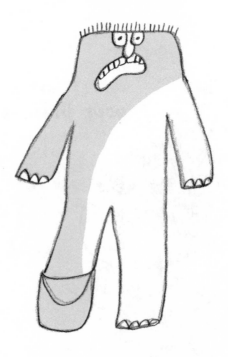

Police help me,
my foot is stuck in a bucket.

Knock knock.
Who's there?

Kent.

Kent who?

Kent you tell by my voice?

Knock knock.
Who's there?

Isabel.
Isabel who?

Isabel not working?

Knock knock.
Who's there?

Cow go.

Cow go who?

No, cow
go moo!

Knock knock.
Who's there?
Money.

Money who?

Money is hurting. I need to
sit down, so let me in!

Knock knock.
Who's there?

Teddy.

Teddy who?

Teddy is a great day for love.
Will you marry me?

Knock knock.
Who's there?

Barbie.

Barbie who?

Barbie-Q!

Knock knock.
Who's there?

Olive.
Olive who?

Olive you!

Knock knock.
Who's there?

Alaska.

Alaska who?

Alaska the question just one
more time: Do you want to buy
this cactus or not?

Knock knock.
Who's there?

Luke.

Luke who?

Luke through the keyhole and you'll find out!

Knock knock.
Who's there?

Mikey.

Mikey who?

*Mikey doesn't fit,
let me in!*

Knock knock.
Who's there?

Abby.
Abby who?

Abby, C, D, E, F, G!

Knock knock.
Who's there?

Razor.

Razor who?

Razor hands! This is a stickup!

Knock knock.
Who's there?

Cash.

Cash who?

No thanks, I prefer peanuts!

Knock knock.
Who's there?

A little old lady.

A little old
lady who?

I didn't know you could yodel!

Knock knock.
Who's there?

Avenue.

Avenue who?

Avenue heard my voice
before? It's me!

Knock knock.
Who's there?

Wooden shoe.
Wooden shoe who?

Wooden shoe like to hear another
knock knock joke?

Knock knock.
Who's there?

Ben.

Ben who?

Ben knocking for 20 minutes!
Let me in!

Knock knock.
Who's there

Amy.

Amy who?

Amy-fraid I've just forgotten.

Knock knock.
Who's there?

Dishes.
Dishes who?

Dishes a lovely day,
don't you think?

Knock knock.
Who's there?

Adore.

Adore who?

Adore just waiting to be
opened!

Knock knock.
Who's there?

Ya.

Ya who?

What are you so excited about?
It's just me.

Knock knock.
Who's there?

Tank.
Tank who?

You're welcome.

Knock knock.
Who's there?

Noah.

Noah who?

Noah decent mechanic?
My car has broken down!

Knock knock.
Who's there?

Alec.

Alec who?

Alec-tricity!

Knock knock.
Who's there?

Mango.

Mango who?

**Mango up and mango down.
Man stuck in elevator!**

Knock knock.
Who's there?

Mike.

Mike who?

**Mike car is on
fire! Help!**

Knock knock.
Who's there?

Water.

Water who?

**Water you doing?
Just open the door!**

Knock knock.
Who's there?

Says.

Says who?

Says me, that's who!

Knock knock.
Who's there?

Canoe.

Canoe who?

Canoe come out and play,
I'm bored!

Knock knock.
Who's there?

Amanda.

Amanda who?

**Amanda fix yer toilet.
I'm da plumber!**

Knock knock.
Who's there?

Kenya.

Kenya who?

*Kenya kindly open the door
right now? I'm hungry!*

Knock knock.
Who's there?

Orange.

Orange who?

Orange you going to let me in?

Knock knock.
Who's there?

Philip.

Philip who?

*Philip this mug right now,
I need more coffee!*

Knock knock.
Who's there?

Denial.

Denial who?

Denial is a river in Egypt.

Knock knock.
Who's there?

Alex.

Alex who?

Alex-plain later,
can't talk right now!

Knock knock.
Who's there?

Russian.

Russian who?

*Russian around is
exhausting!!
I need a rest!*

Knock knock.
Who's there?

Donut.

Donut who?

Donut ask, it's a secret!

Knock knock.
Who's there?

Witches.

Witches who?

Witches the way home?
We're lost!

Knock knock.
Who's there?

Dozen.

Dozen who?

Dozen anyone want to let us in?

Knock knock.
Who's there?

Euripides.

Euripides who?

Euripides jeans, you pay for them!

Knock knock.
Who's there?

Thermos.

Thermos who?

Thermos be a better way of getting in than just standing here knocking like an idiot!

Knock knock.
Who's there?

Hairy.

Hairy who?

**Hairy up, the train
leaves in five minutes!**

Knock knock.
Who's there?

Anita.

Anita who?

Anita borrow some eggs for
this cake please.

Knock knock.
Who's there?

Theresa.

Theresa who?

Theresa scary
spider out here!
Let me in!

Knock knock.
Who's there?

Orange.

Orange who?

Orange you glad to see me!?!

Knock knock.
Who's there?

Banana.

Banana who?

Banana split! Bye!!!

Knock knock.
Who's there?

Iran.

Iran who?

Iran all the way here to see you! Let me in!!

Knock knock.
Who's there?

Armageddon.

Armageddon who?

*Armageddon a bit bored,
kindly let me in.*

Knock knock.
Who's there?

Sadie.

Sadie who?

Sadie magic word and watch me disappear!

Knock knock.
Who's there?

Beets.

Beets who?

Beets me!

Knock knock.
Who's there?

Will.

Will who?

*Will you please open the door.
It's freezing out here!*

Knock knock.
Who's there?

Justin.

Justin who?

Justin the neighborhood. Thought I'd pop in for a cup of tea.

Knock knock.
Who's there?

Jamaican.

Jamaican who?

Jamaican omelette or a pizza? I'm hungry!

Knock knock.
Who's there?

Norway.

Norway who?

Norway through the back—let me in the front!

Knock knock.
Who's there?

Egg.

Egg who?

Eggcellent weather, isn't it!

50

Knock knock.
Who's there?

Stopwatch.

Stopwatch who?

Stopwatch-ya-doing
and let me in.
It's raining out here!

Knock knock.
Who's there?

Orange.

Orange who?

Orange you glad I didn't say banana?

Knock knock.
Who's there?

Beef.

Beef who?

Beef-ore I start getting annoyed, let me in!

Knock knock.
Who's there?

Andrew.

Andrew who?

Andrew all over the wall.
She's in biiiiig trouble.

Knock knock.
Who's there?

Bella.

Bella who?

Bella not-a-working so
I ring-a the doorbell.

Knock knock.
Who's there?

Zealous.

Zealous who?

Zealous you know about me ze better.

Knock knock.
Who's there?

Victor.

Victor who?

Victor his trousers on the way over.

Knock knock.
Who's there?

Venice.

Venice who?

Venice the best time to come by for tea and cake?

Knock knock.
Who's there?

Peas.

Peas who?

Peas be with you, my friend!

Knock knock.
Who's there?

Cereal.

Cereal who?

Cereal honor to meet you!

Knock knock.
Who's there?

Alec.

Alec who?

Alec tea, but I don't like coffee.

Knock knock.
Who's there?

Sue.

Sue who?

Sue-percalifragilisticexpialidocious!

Knock knock.
Who's there?

Jelly.

Jelly who?

Jelly-sy gets you nowhere!

Knock knock.
Who's there?

Marmalade.

Marmalade who?

Marmalade an egg!

Knock knock.
Who's there?

Wendy.

Wendy who?

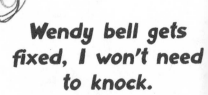

Wendy bell gets
fixed, I won't need
to knock.

Knock knock.
Who's there?

Needle.

Needle who?

Needle love in your life?
Well, here I am!

Knock knock.
Who's there?

Ann.

Ann who?

Anonymous.
You'll never know.

Knock knock.
Who's there?

Caesar.

Caesar who?

Caesar rain cloud?
Storm's a-comin'!

Knock knock.
Who's there?

Butter.

Butter who?

Butter open the door and let me in before I melt!

Knock knock.
Who's there?

Jester.

Jester who?

Jester silly little lady!

Knock knock.
Who's there?

Olive.

Olive who?

*No idea who—
maybe that person
you keep smiling at?*

Knock knock.
Who's there?

Stu.

Stu who?

*Stupid doorbell seems
to be broken.*

Knock knock.
Who's there?

Lettuce.   **Lettuce who?**

Lettuce come in please!

Knock knock.
Who's there?

Herd.

Herd who?

Herd there was a party at your place —can I come in?

Knock knock.
Who's there?

Annetta.

Annetta who?

Annetta catches da fish-a!

Knock knock.
Who's there?

Mikey.

Mikey who?

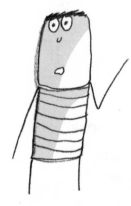

Mikey is lost, that's why
I couldn't let myself in.
Please open up!

Knock knock.
Who's there?

Vincent.

Vincent who?

*Vincent me
here!*

Knock knock.
Who's there?

Ears.

Ears who?

*Ears another
knock knock
joke!*

Knock knock.
Who's there?

Wooden shoe.

Wooden shoe who?

*Wooden shoe like to
share this cake?*

Knock knock.
Who's there?

Fangs.

Fangs who?

Fangs for letting me in at last!

Knock knock.
Who's there?

Ernie.

Ernie who?

Ernie money by workie hard!

Knock knock.
Who's there?

Jeff.

Jeff who?

**Jeff find my cat?
She's lost!**

Knock knock.
Who's there?

Ringo.

Ringo who?

**Ringo round
the roses.**

Knock knock.
Who's there?

Yvonne.

Yvonne who?

Yvonne to be alone?

Knock knock.
Who's there?

Jenny.

Jenny who?

Jenny still hurting or is it better?

Knock knock.
Who's there?

Venice.

Venice who?

Venice your mother
coming home.

Knock knock.
Who's there?

Heart.

Heart who?

Heart to hear what
you're saying—please
speak up!

Knock knock.
Who's there?

Zits.

Zits who?

Zits time to go!

Knock knock.
Who's there?

Taylor.

Taylor who?

Taylor head?
Your call!

Knock knock.
Who's there?

Abel.

Abel who?

Abel to see you through the keyhole!

Knock knock.
Who's there?

William.

William who?

William mind your own business!

Knock knock.
Who's there?

John.

John who?

*John never going to believe
what I have to tell you!*

Knock knock.
Who's there?

Watson.

Watson who?

Watson TV?

Knock knock.
Who's there?

Alison.

Alison who?

Alison to you if you listen to me.

Knock knock.
Who's there?

Tamara.

Tamara who?

Tamara is Friday. Today is
Thursday (I think!)

Knock knock.
Who's there?

Les.

Les who?

Les go to the lake,
I have a boat!

Knock knock.
Who's there?

Zeke.

Zeke who?

Zeke . . . and ye shall find.

Knock knock.
Who's there?

House.

House who?

House you doin'?

Knock knock.
Who's there?

Emma.

Emma who?

Emma bit annoyed that you don't know who I am!

Knock knock.
Who's there?

Barbara.

Barbara who?

Barbara black sheep, have you any wool?

Knock knock.
Who's there?

Ice cream.

Ice cream who?

Ice cream if you
don't let me in
RIGHT NOW!

Knock knock.
Who's there?

Waiter.

Waiter who?

Waiter minute—
is this even the
right house?

Knock knock.
Who's there?

Adore.

Adore who?

Adore stands between us!
Please open it immediately!

Knock knock.
Who's there?

X.

X who?

X for breakfast!
Scrambled, fried,
or boiled?

Knock knock.
Who's there?

Jim.

Jim who?

Jim mind if I come in?

Knock knock.
Who's there?

Leaf.

Leaf who?

Leaf me alone!

Knock knock.
Who's there?

Howard.

Howard who?

Howard you like a lovely cup of tea?

Knock knock.
Who's there?

Earl.

Earl who?

Earl be very glad when you finally let me in!

Knock knock.
Who's there?

Alfie.

Alfie who?

Alfie terrible if you don't let me in!

Knock knock.
Who's there?

Abby.

Abby who?

Abby stung me—
look how swollen my nose is!

Knock knock.
Who's there?

Paul.

Paul who?

Paul-ice. Put your
hands in the air!

Knock knock.
Who's there?

Nun.

Nun who?

Nun of your
beeswax.

Knock knock.
Who's there?

Tennis.

Tennis who?

Tennis 5 + 5.
Everybody knows that!

Knock knock.
Who's there?

Eggs.

Eggs who?

Eggcellent! And how are you?

Knock knock.
Who's there?

Oscar.

Oscar who?

Oscar weird question,
get a weird answer.

Knock knock.
Who's there?

Russell.

Russell who?

Russell up a quick lettuce salad
please. I'm starving!

Knock knock.
Who's there?

Sacha.

Sacha who?

*Sacha hot day! Please can
I come in and get a glass
of cold water?*

Knock knock.
Who's there?

Canoe.

Canoe who?

Canoe help me with this cactus? It's really heavy.

Knock knock.
Who's there?

Major.

Major who?

Major answer the door, hahahahahahaha!

Knock knock.
Who's there?

Snow.

Snow who?

Snow-body.

Knock knock.
Who's there?

Quack.

Quack who?

Quack another duck joke and
I'll call the joke police!

Knock knock.
Who's there?

Max.

Max who?

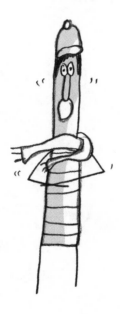

**Max a big difference if
you open up right now. It's
freezing out here!**

Knock knock.
Who's there?

Utah.

Utah who?

Utah one who locked ta door in ta first place—let me in!

Knock knock.
Who's there?

Rob.

Rob who?

Robbers don't knock!

Knock knock.
Who's there?

Radio.

Radio who?

Radio not,
here I come,
you can't hide!

99

Knock knock.
Who's there?

Teresa.

Teresa who?

Teresa green. So is grass!

Knock knock.
Who's there?

Bed.

Bed who?

Bed you can't guess who this is!

Knock knock.
Who's there?

Hugo.

Hugo who?

Hugo-ing to open up or not?

Knock knock.
Who's there?

Water.

Water who?

Water rude way to
answer the door!

Knock knock.
Who's there?

Dozen.

Dozen who?

Dozen anyone wanna let me in?

Knock knock.
Who's there?

Chick.

Chick who?

Chick if your oven is on— there's smoke coming out of your roof!

103

Knock knock.
Who's there?

Avenue.

Avenue who?

**Avenue learned to be polite
and let people in?**

Knock knock.
Who's there?

Claire.

Claire who?

Claire the way, I'm in a hurry!

Knock knock.
Who's there?

Sadie.

Sadie who?

Sadie magic word
and I'll turn myself
into a bunny.

Knock knock.
Who's there?

Juno.

Juno who?

Juno how long we've
been waiting out here?

Knock knock.
Who's there?

Double.

Double who?

Double U!

Knock knock.
Who's there?

Zany.

Zany who?

Zany one home?

Knock knock.
Who's there?

Sarah.

Sarah who?

Sarah 'nother way in?

Knock knock.
Who's there?

Lionel.

Lionel who?

Lionel get you nowhere.

Knock knock.
Who's there?

Walter.

Walter who?

Walter wall carpeting would go well in this room.

Knock knock.
Who's there?

Luke.

Luke who?

c'est moi

Luke through the keyhole and you'll see!

Knock knock.
Who's there?

Heidi.

Heidi who?

Heidi-cided to come say hi!

Knock knock.
Who's there?

Ivor.

Ivor who?

Ivor message for you.

Knock knock.
Who's there?

Kent.

Kent who?

Kent you tell by
my voice?

Knock knock.
Who's there?

Francis.

Francis who?

Francis on the other
side of the ocean!

Knock knock.
Who's there?

Nun.

Nun who?

Nun-ya business!

Knock knock.
Who's there?

Jess.

Jess who?

Jess me and my shadow.

Knock knock.
Who's there?

Ivan.

Ivan who?

Ivan to be alone.

Knock knock.
Who's there?

Keith.

Keith who?

Keith me kwik!

115

Knock knock.
Who's there?

Yvonne.

Yvonne who?

Yvonne to be alone.

Knock knock.
Who's there?

Linda.

Linda who?

Linda hand, this is really heavy!

Knock knock.
Who's there?

Manny.

Manny who?

**Manny, manny people
ask me that!**

Knock knock.
Who's there?

Comb.

Comb who?

Comb down and I'll tell you!

Knock knock.
Who's there?

Olga.

Olga who?

**Olga way after you give
me a treat!**

Knock knock.
Who's there?

Ollie.

Ollie who?

Ollie time you ask the same question: "Who's there?" Why don't you just open the door?

Have you laughed aloud at The World's Best Jokes for Kids VOLUMES 1, 2, and 3?

The World's Best Knock Knock Jokes for Kids Volume 4

Andrews McMeel Publishing
a division of Andrews McMeel Universal
1130 Walnut Street, Kansas City, Missouri 64106

www.andrewsmcmeel.com

19 20 21 22 23 VEP 10 9 8 7 6 5 4 3 2 1

ISBN: 978-1-5248-5332-7

Library of Congress Control Number: 2019940387

Made by:
Versa Press Inc.
Address and location of manufacturer:
1465 Spring Bay Road/Route 26
East Peoria, IL 61611
1st Printing—9/9/19

For lots more funny, silly, and random jokes,
visit us online:
www.lastlemon.com/silliness
www.instagram.com/silliness.is
www.facebook.com/silliness.is

Send us a joke. If we like it,
we'll illustrate it:
www.lastlemon.com/silliness/submit

ATTENTION: SCHOOLS AND BUSINESSES

Andrews McMeel books are available at quantity discounts with
bulk purchase for educational, business, or sales promotional use.
For information, please e-mail the Andrews McMeel Publishing
Special Sales Department: specialsales@amuniversal.com.